A Sister's Hand

By: DJP Family Productions

Copyright © 2012
www.djpfamilyproductions.com

Author Name: DJP Family Productions
All rights reserved.

ISBN: 9781094602219

WHAT DO YOU THINK?

1. Looking at the cover, what do you think this book might be about?

2. What do you think will happen in the story?

3. Why do you think the author gave this book that title?

4. After reading the blurb, what is something you are looking forward to discovering in this book?

5. How do you think this story will end?

6. What is a problem that you think could occur in this story?

7. Parents/Kids, tell us what you think before you read.

Like our Facebook and message us your answers to the questions listed above.

https://www.facebook.com/djpfamilyproductions/

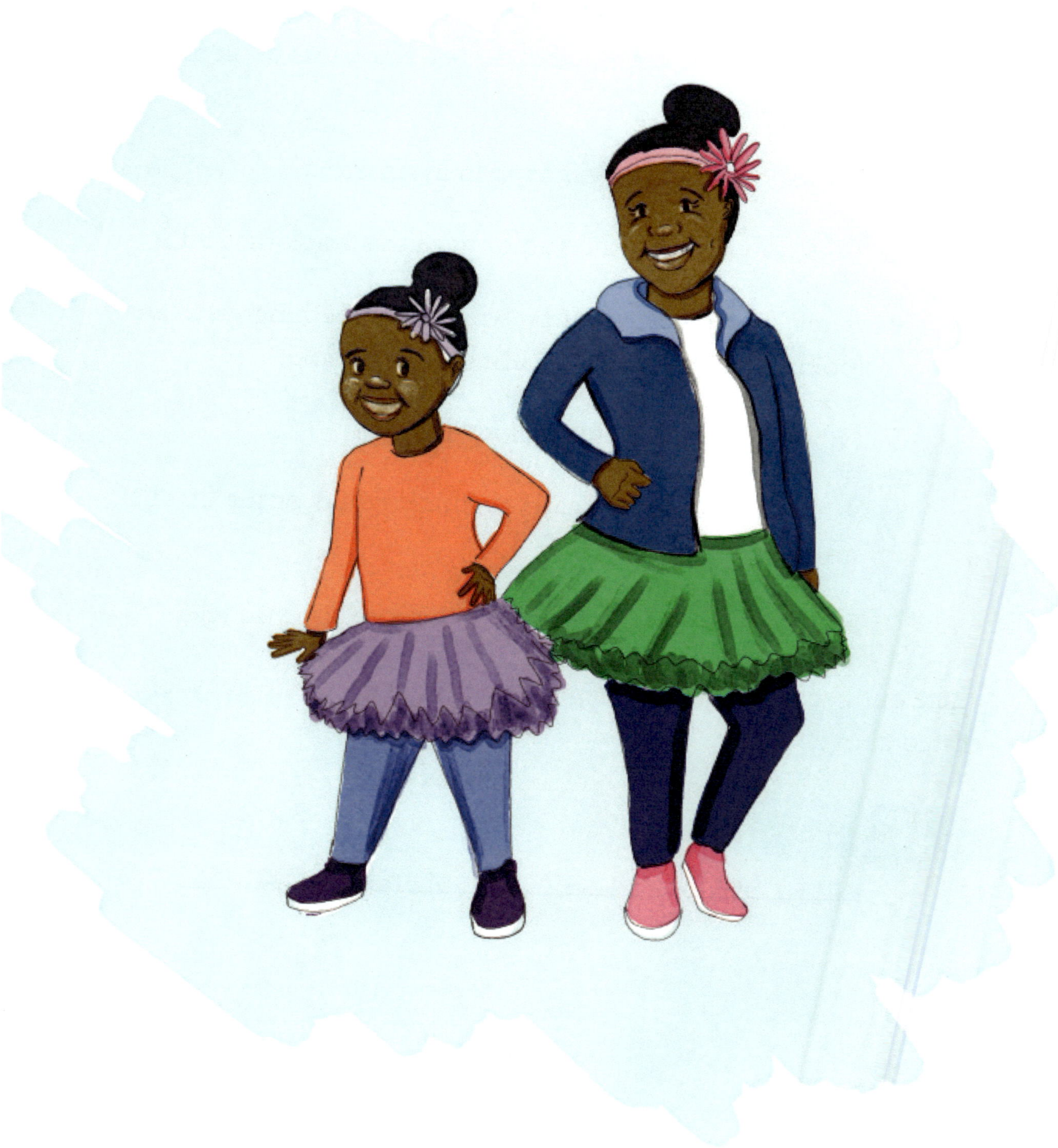

Jaimie and Jordyn are sisters. Jaimie is 11 years old, and Jordyn is 6 years old. Jordyn admires Jaimie. They enjoy spending time together and sometimes they even dress alike.

One Saturday afternoon, Jaimie and Jordyn prepared for a trip to the mall. Jaimie enjoyed helping her little sister Jordyn get ready, but Jordyn didn't want any help. Now that Jordyn was growing up, she wanted to
do things by herself.

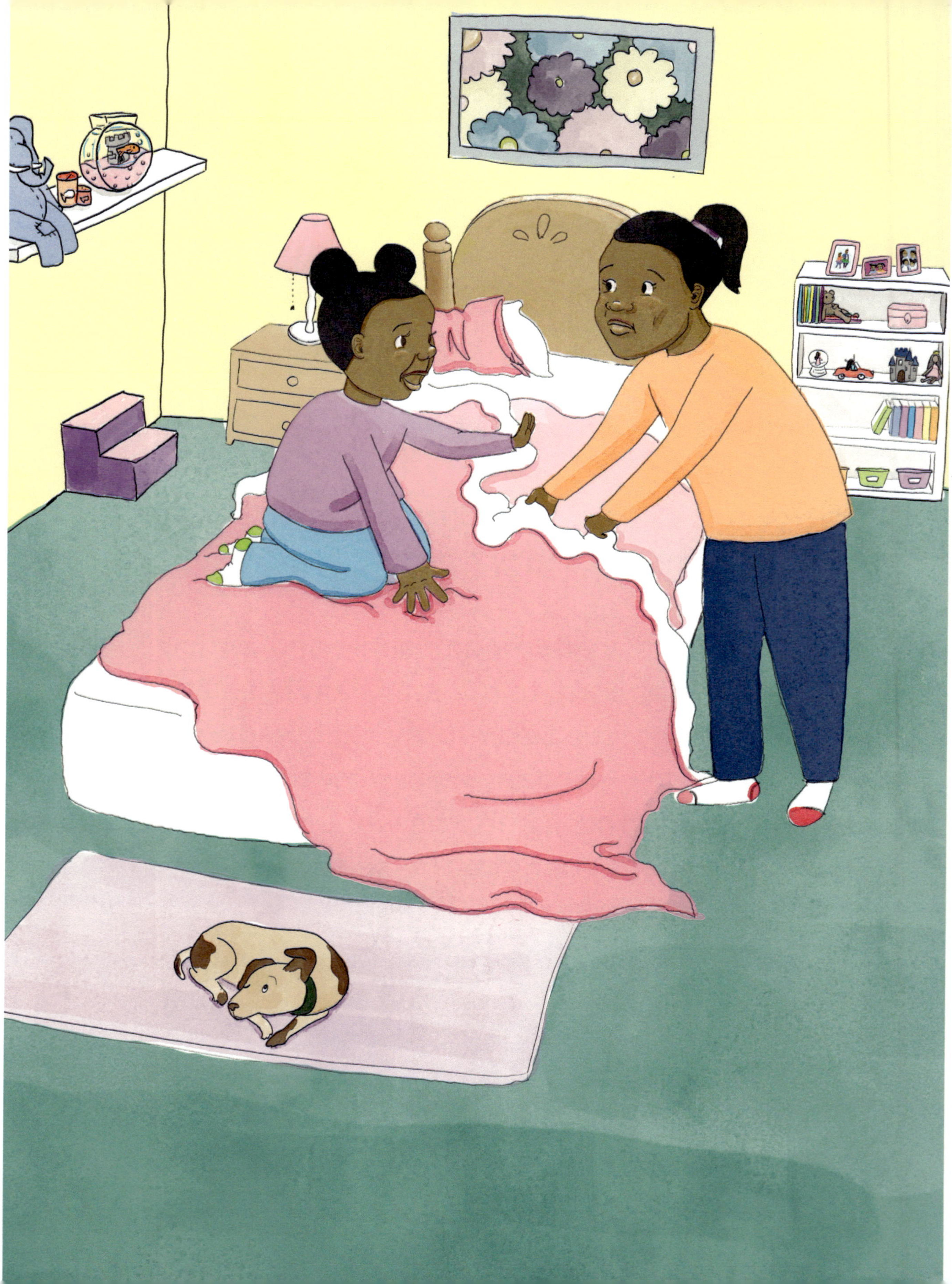

Jaimie tried to help Jordyn make her bed.

"No, thank you, Jaimie," Jordyn said. "I can make my own bed. I'm a big girl now."

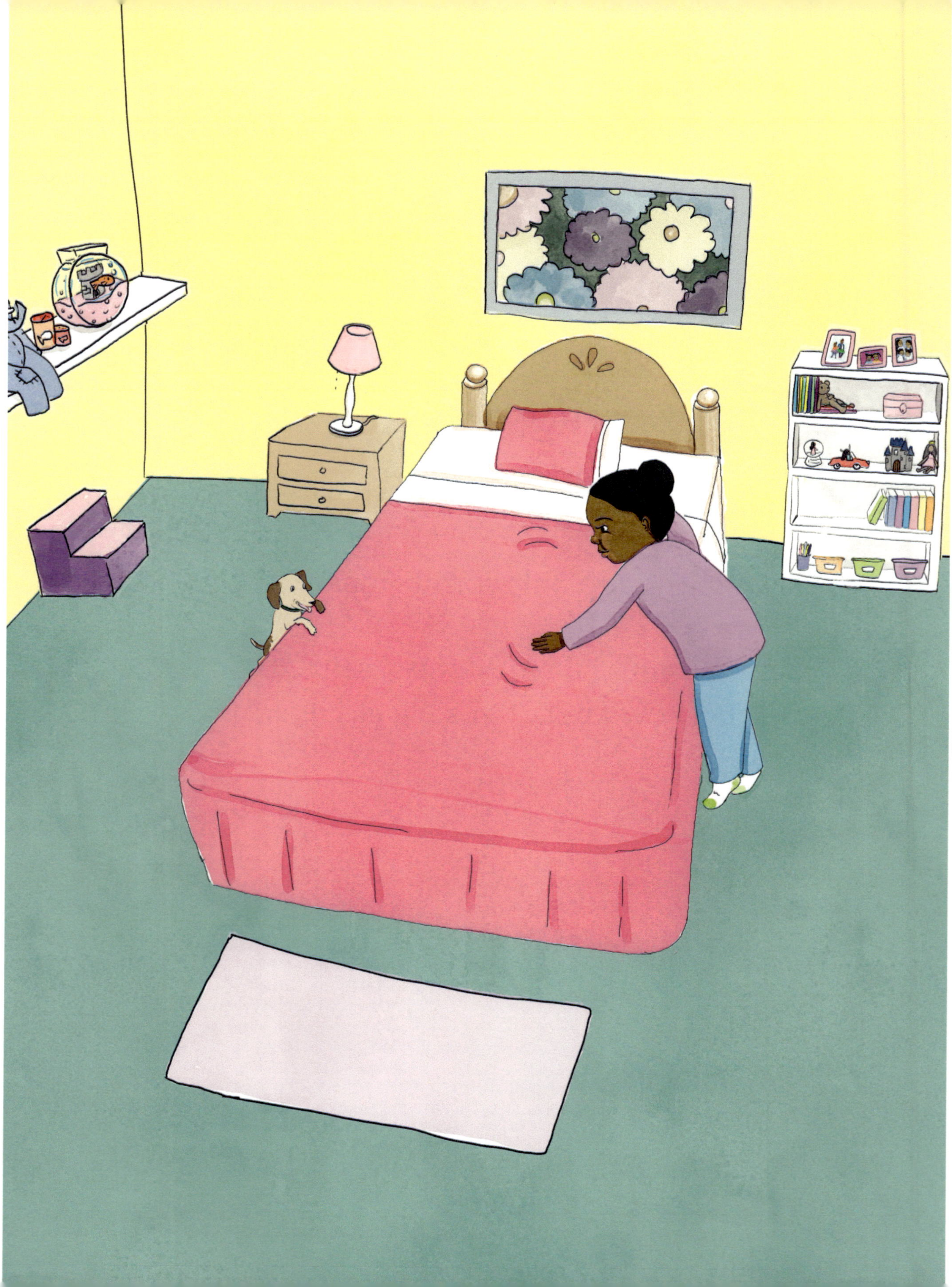

She moved Jaimie's hand away
and fixed her own bed.

"Okay, Jordyn," Jaimie said nicely.
"I just wanted to help."

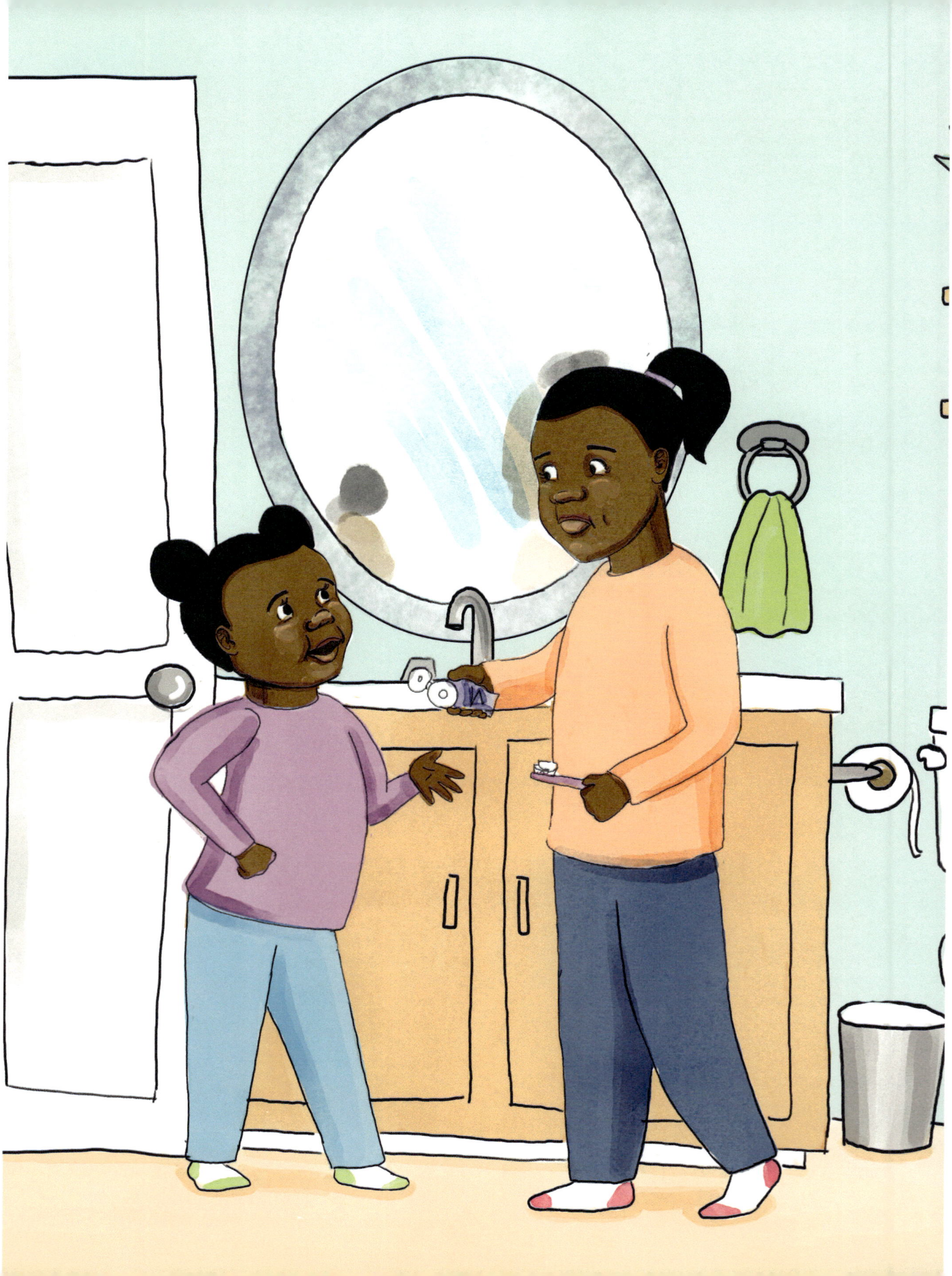

Next, the sisters went to the restroom to brush their teeth. Jaimie tried to help Jordyn put toothpaste on her toothbrush.

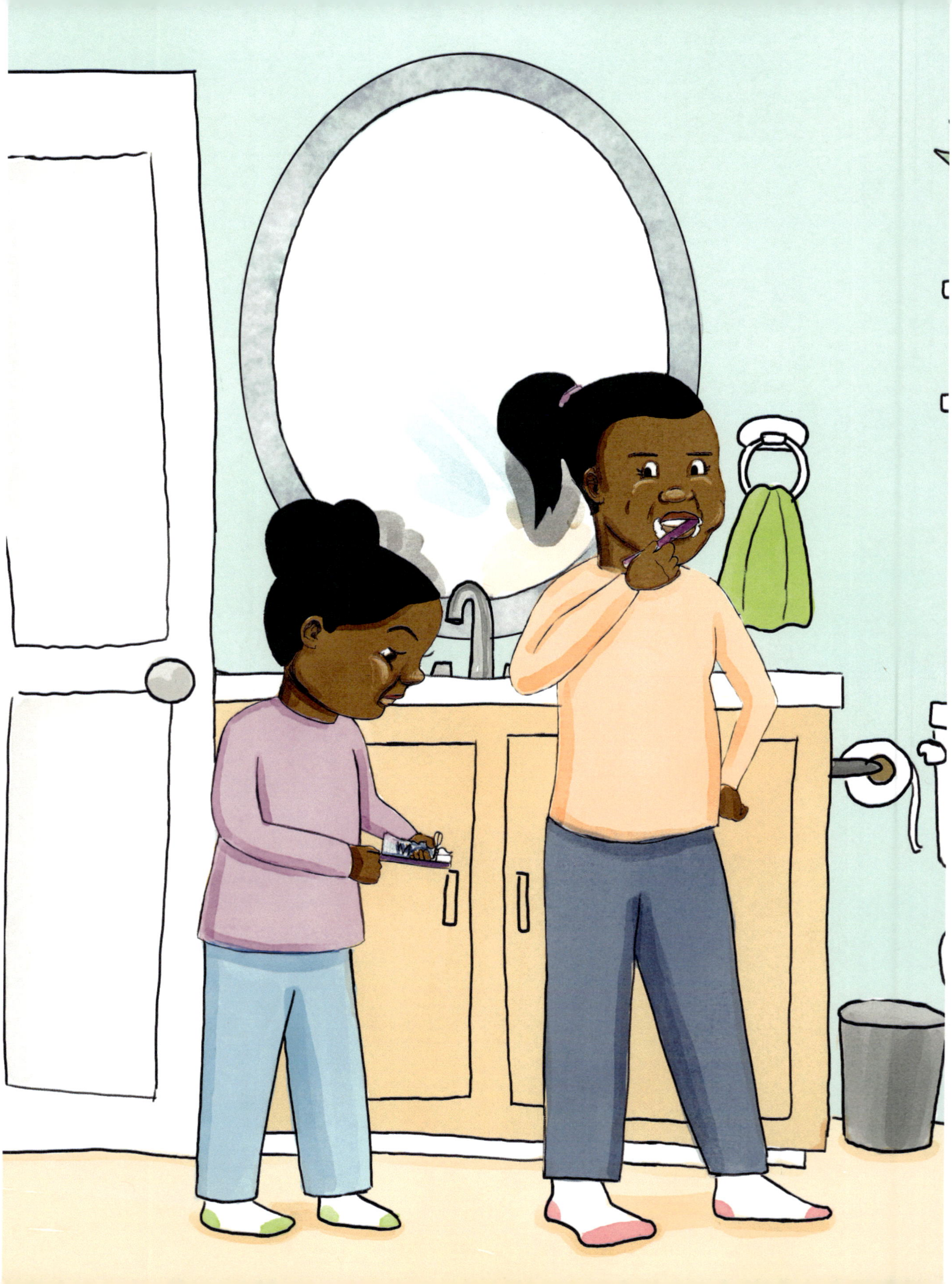

"No, thank you, Jaimie," Jordyn said. "I can put the toothpaste on the brush. I'm a big girl now."

Jaimie took a step back. "Okay, Jordyn. I just wanted to help."

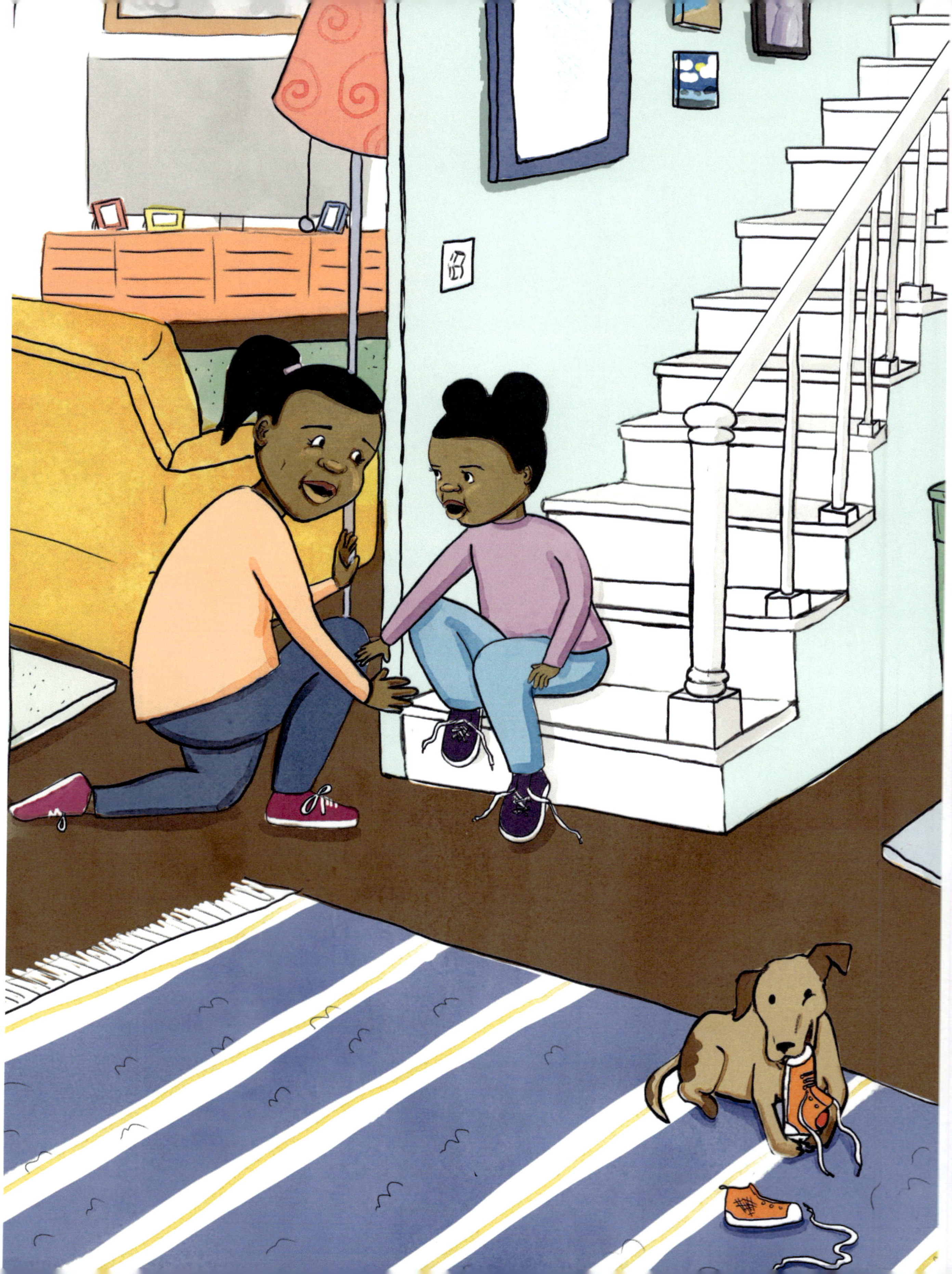

Next, the sisters headed to the steps to put on their shoes. Jaimie tried to help Jordyn tie her shoes like she did every day since
she could walk.

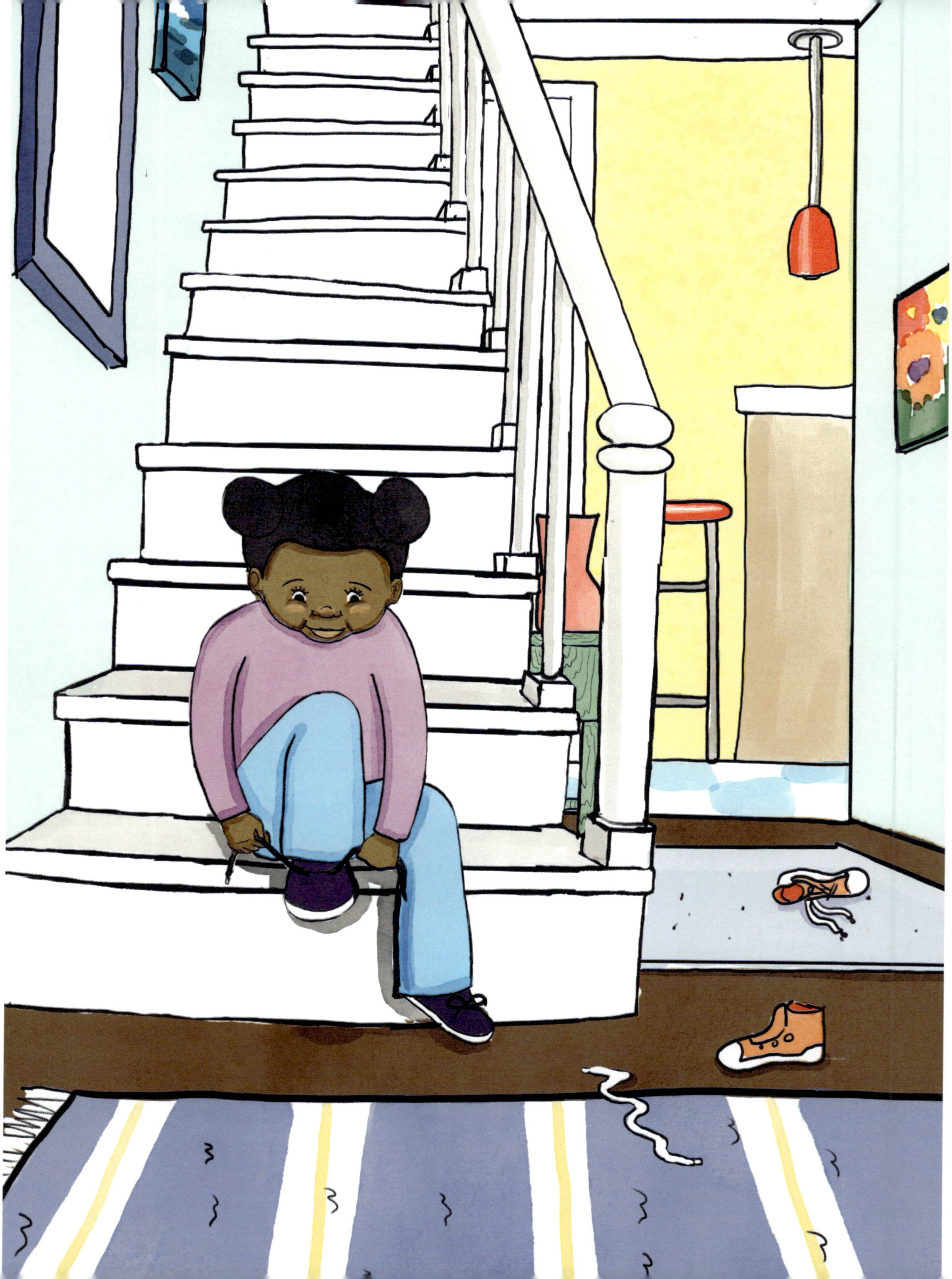

"No, thank you," Jordyn said as she grabbed her shoestrings. "I can tie my shoes.
I'm a big girl now."

"Okay, Jordyn," Jaimie replied.
"I just wanted to help."

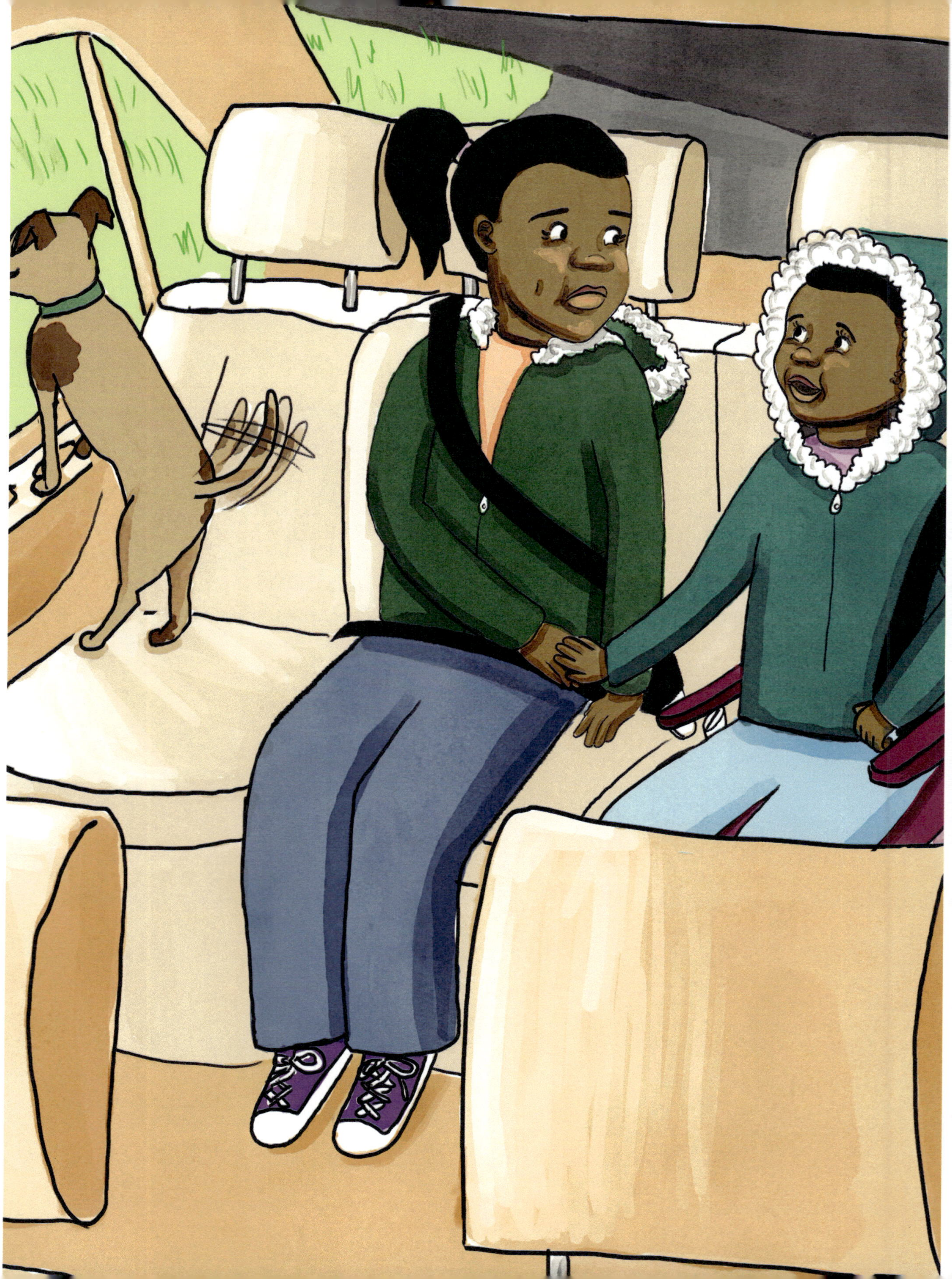

The sisters loaded the car to ride to the mall. Jaimie tried to help Jordyn buckle her seatbelt like she always did, but this time Jordyn stopped her, once again, to do it herself.

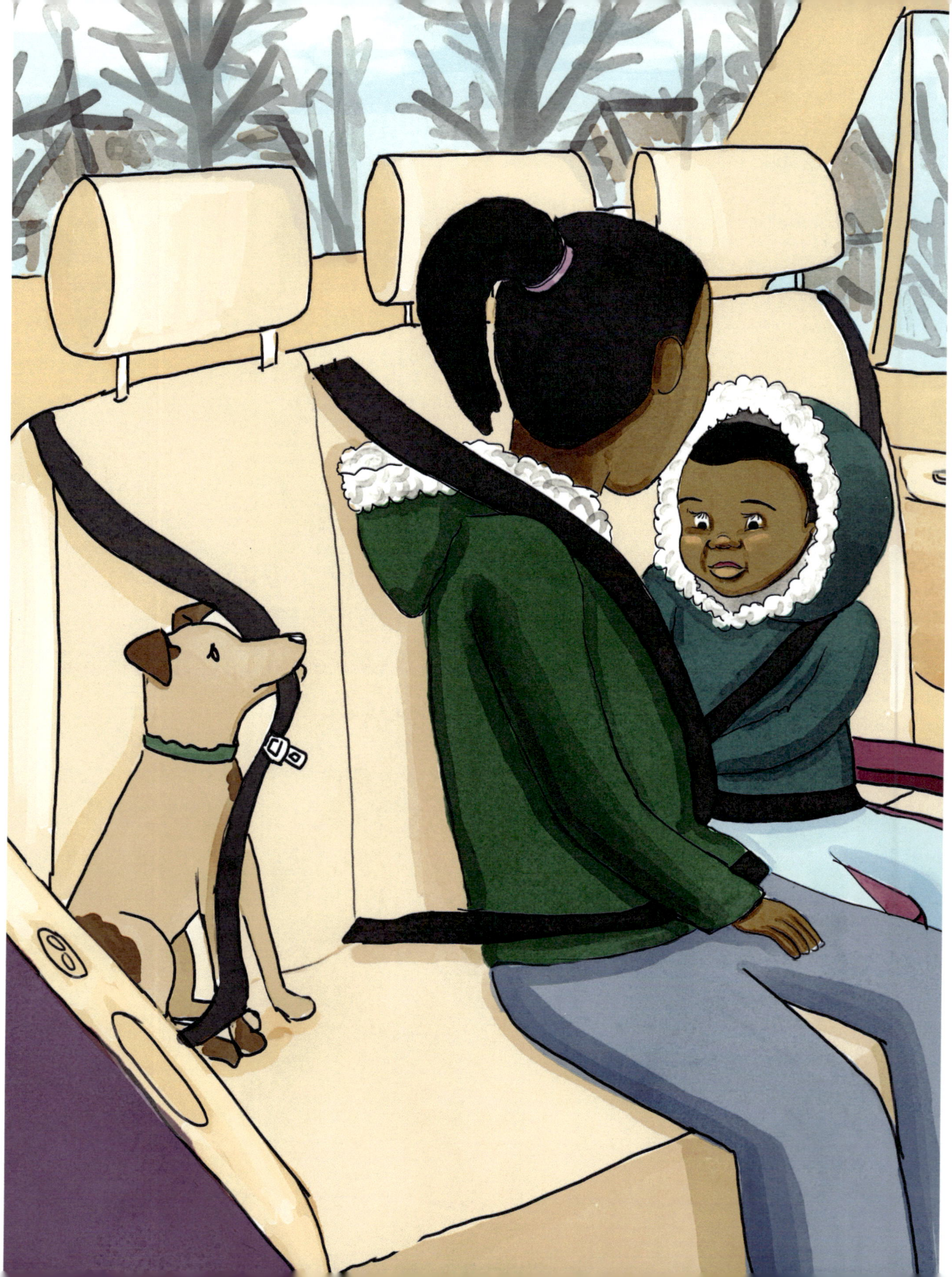

"No, thank you, Jaimie," Jordyn said. "I can buckle my own seatbelt. I'm a big girl now." Jordyn reached down and buckled her seatbelt.

"Okay, Jordyn," Jaimie said.
"I just wanted to help."

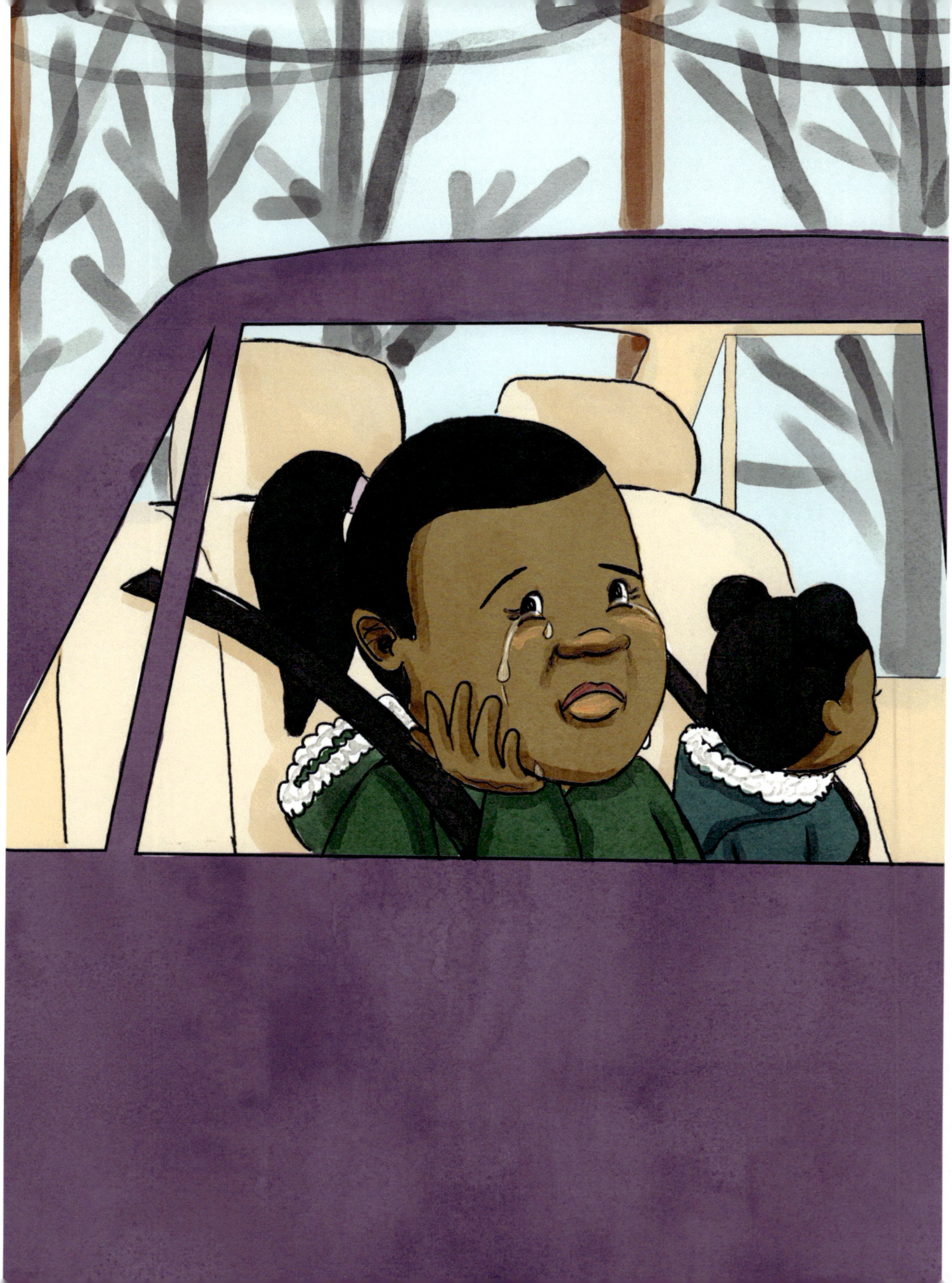

Jaimie was sad that Jordyn did not want or need her help anymore. She looked out the window and tried not to cry.

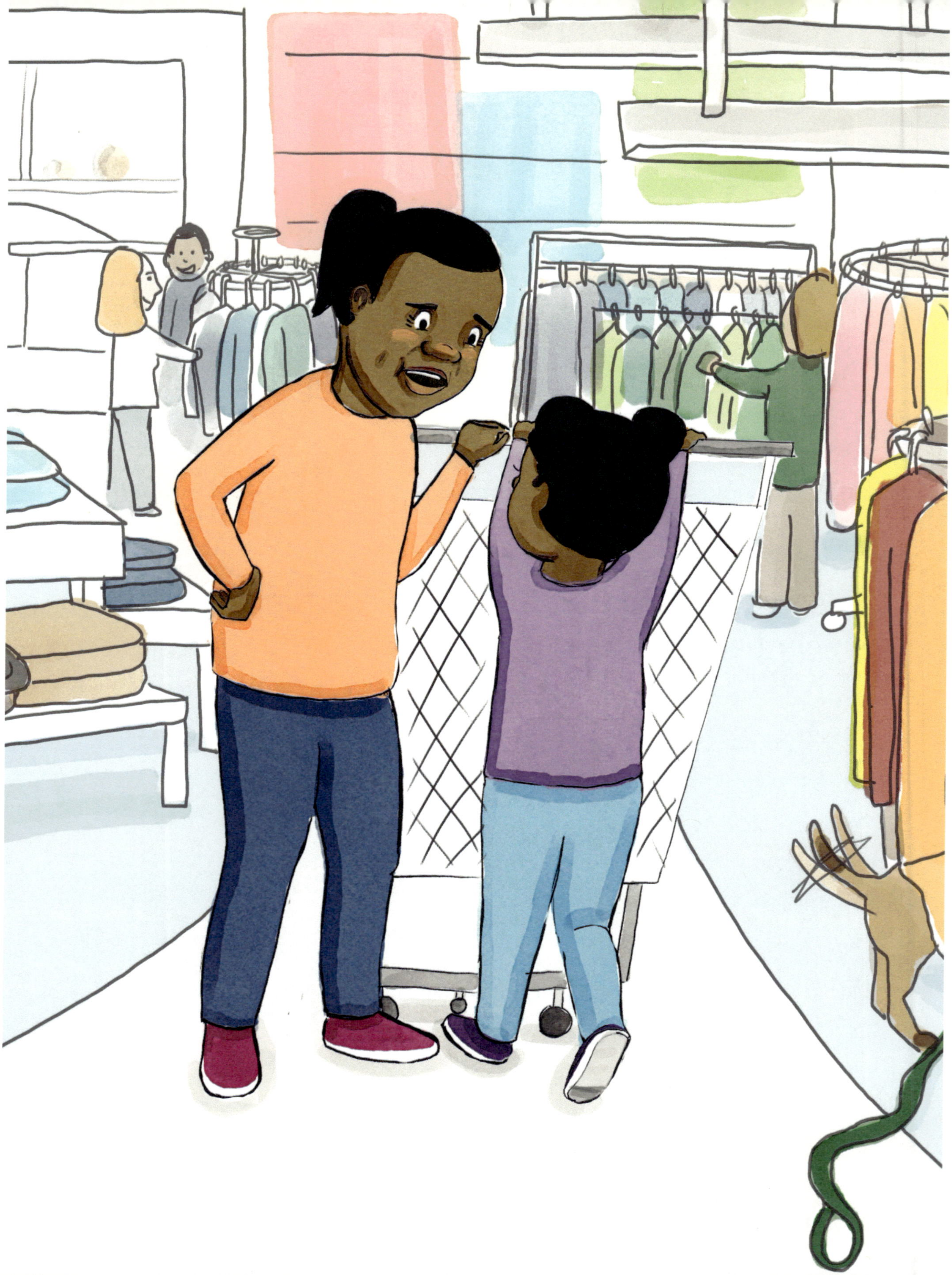

Once in the store, the sisters walked to get a shopping cart. Jordyn usually rode in the shopping cart while Jaimie pushed.

"Okay, Jordyn. I'll hold it while you climb in. Be careful."

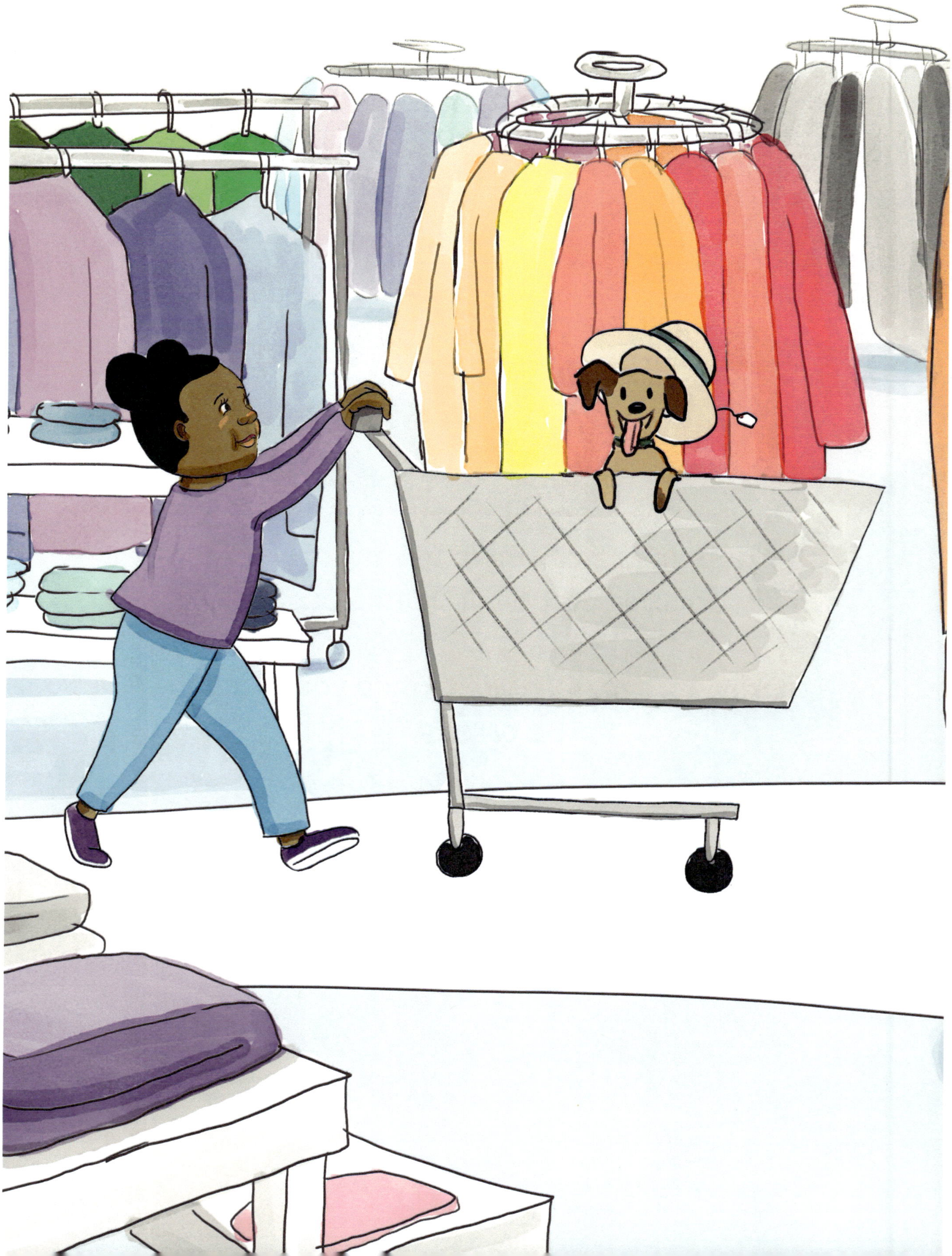

"No, thank you, Jaimie," Jordyn said and grabbed the cart. "I want to push the cart, not get inside. I'm a big girl now."

Jaimie was not sure about that idea. "Okay, Jordyn, but you can barely see over the handle."

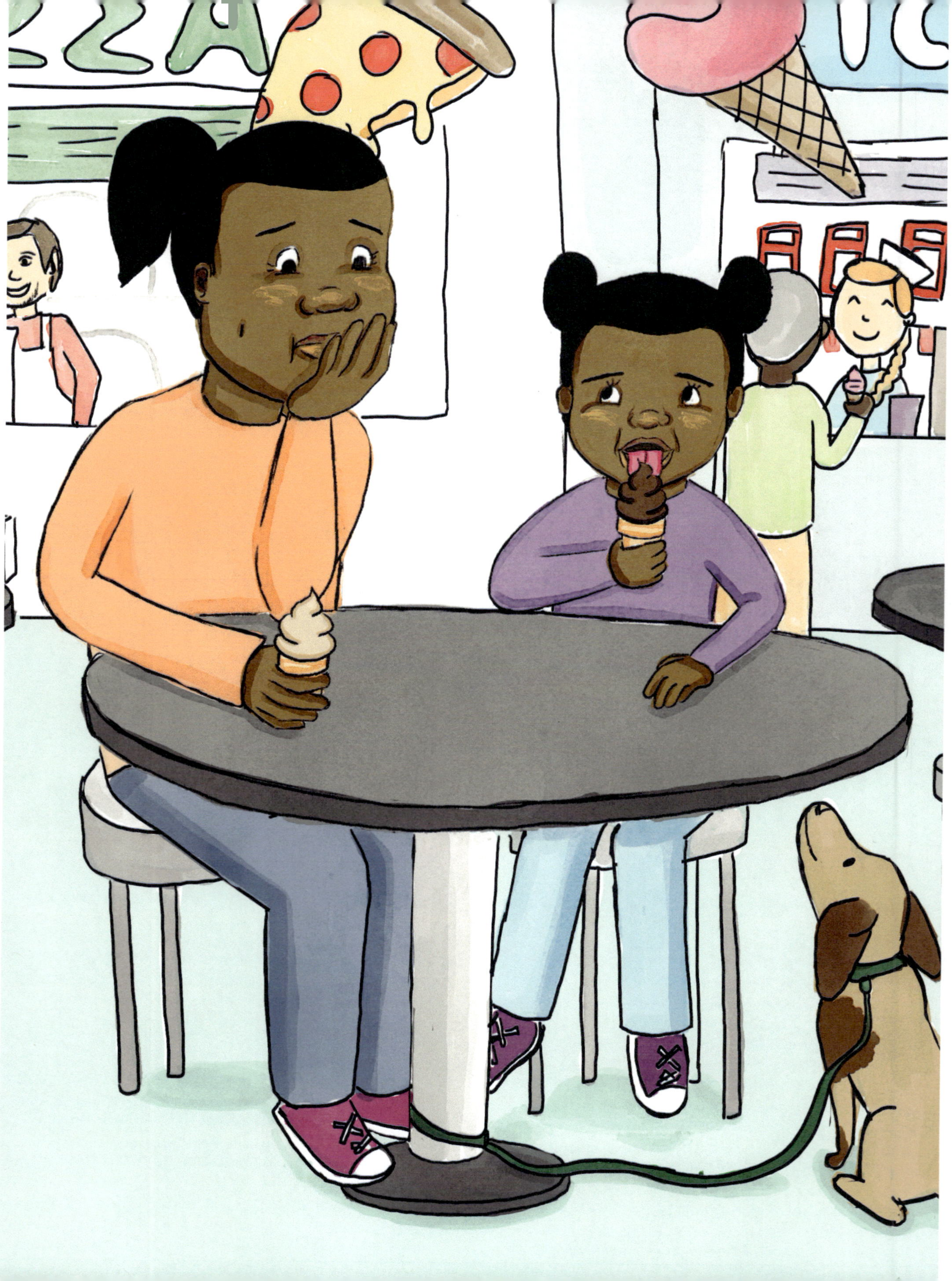

The sisters walked the mall and finally stopped for ice cream. Jaimie was still a little sad from Jordyn not allowing her to help her most of the day.

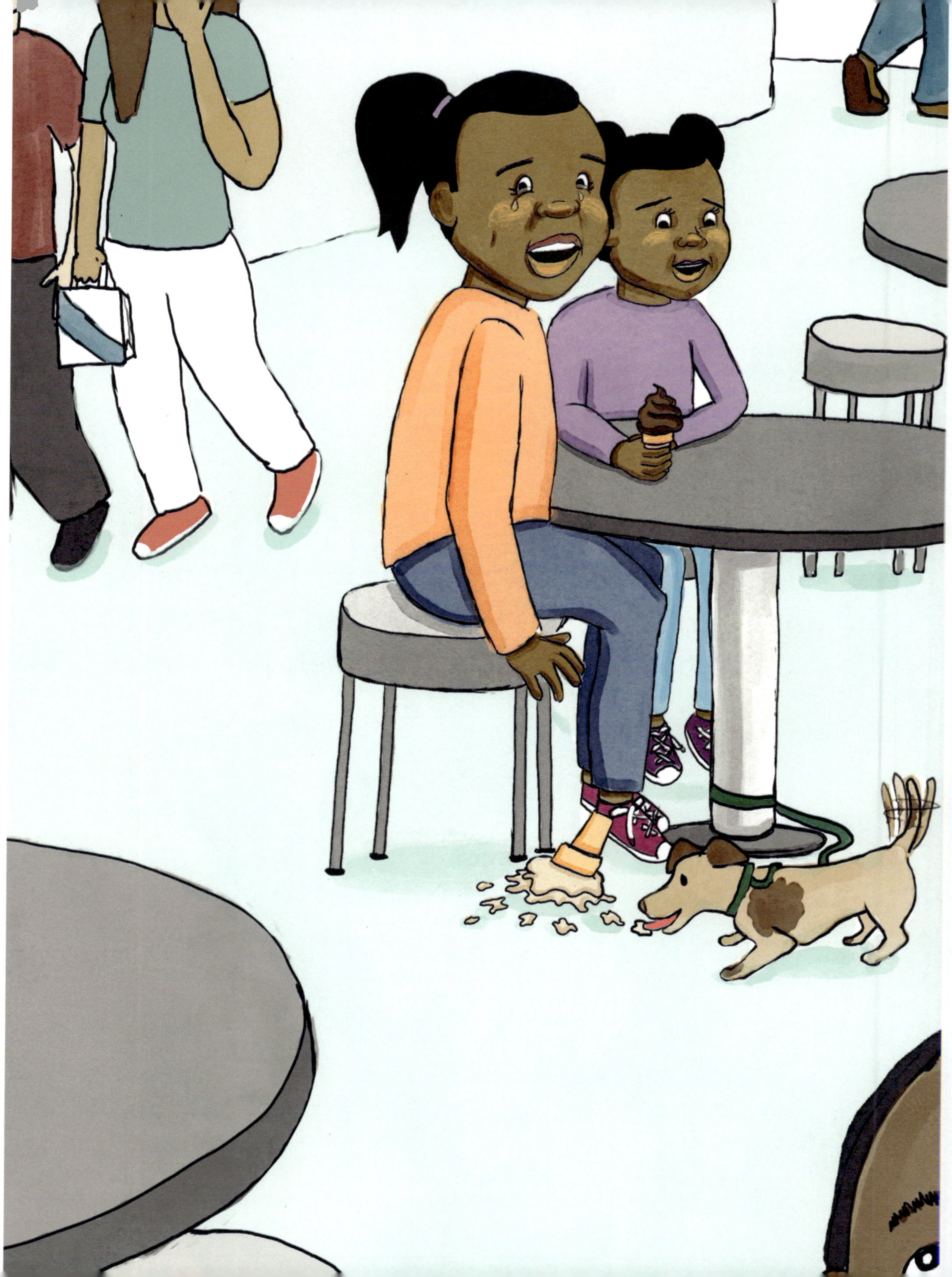

While Jaimie daydreamed about how different Jordyn acted, she accidentally let her ice cream cone slip out of her hand.

"Oh no, my ice cream has dropped!" cried Jaimie. "First, my sister doesn't need me anymore, and now my ice cream."

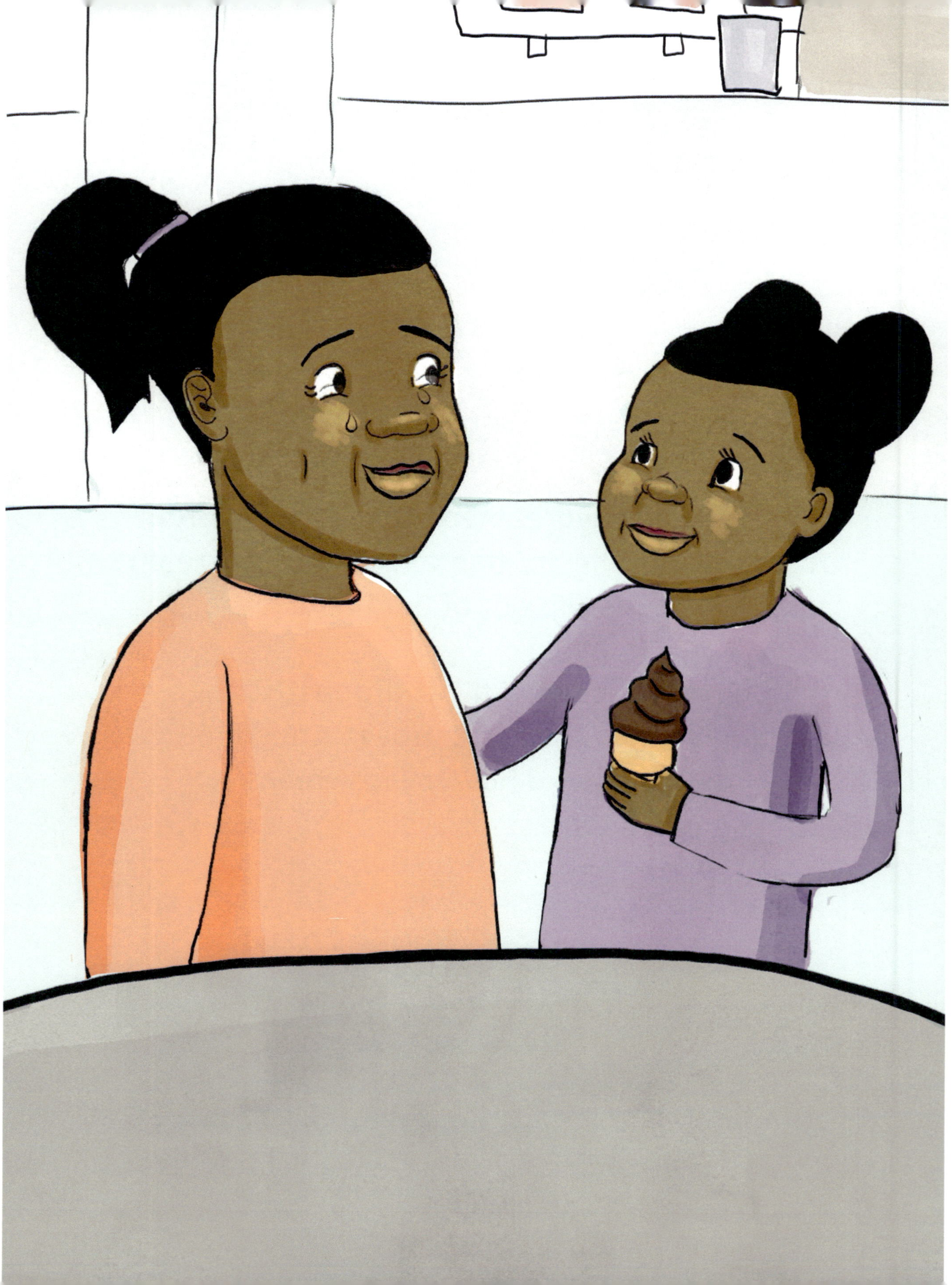

Jordyn put her hand on her big sister's arm. "Jaimie, please don't be sad. I will always need you. You are the best big sister. We can share my ice cream."

Jaimie smiled at Jordyn's offer to share her ice cream.

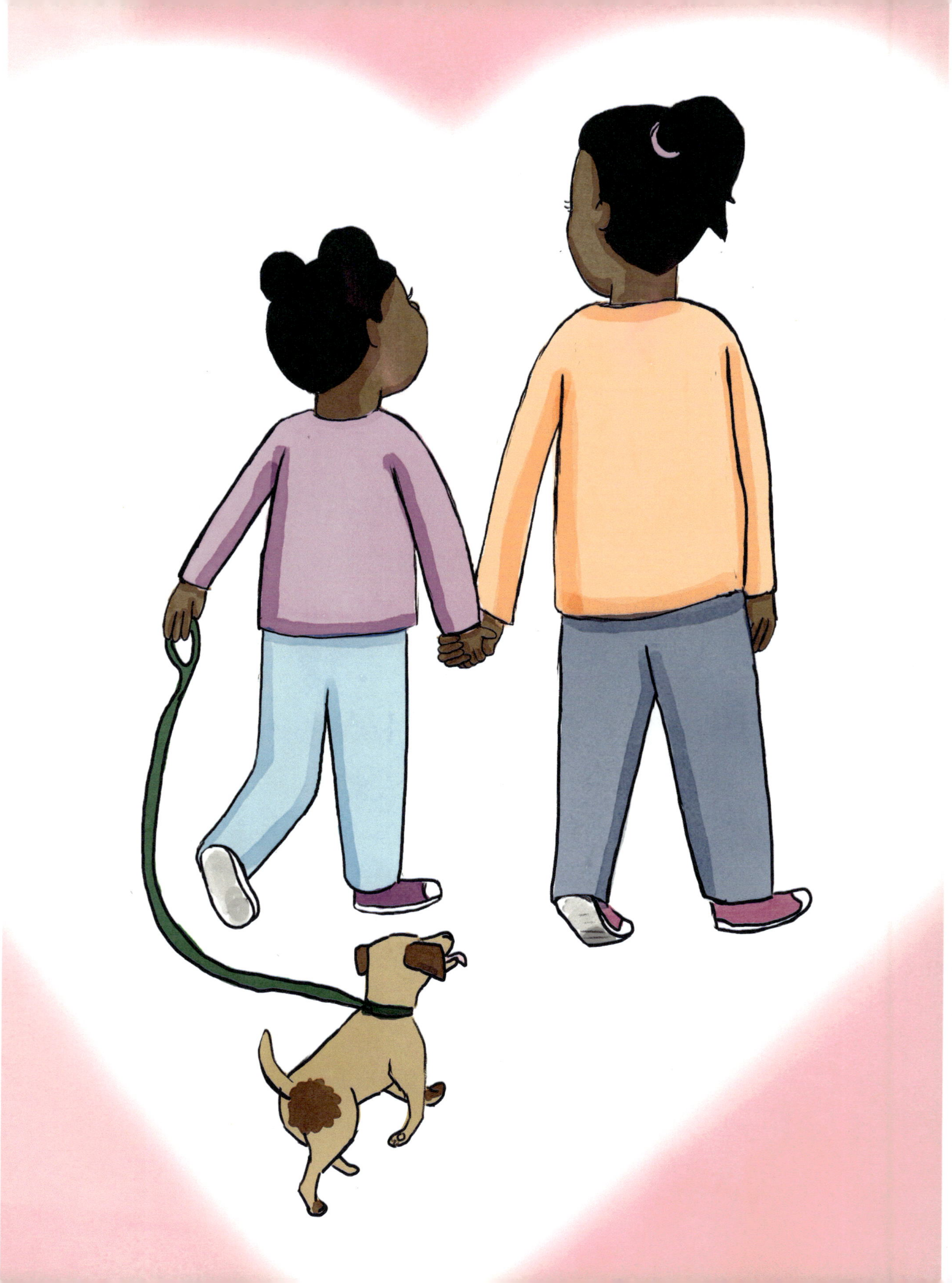

The sisters walked the mall hand and hand for the rest of the afternoon. Jaimie learned that little sisters grow up. And Jordyn learned she will always need her big sister.

ABOUT THE AUTHORS

DJP Family Productions is owned and operated by Diego and Dezirae. Diego and Dezirae are brother and sister who live in Maryland. Aspiring to make their dreams come true, they set a goal to write books about their life and share it with the world. They have put serious effort to not only be great storytellers, but young business owners.

WHAT DO YOU THINK?

1. Was Jaimie right to feel sad?

2. Have you ever tried to help someone who didn't want your help?

3. Have you met anyone that reminds you of Jaimie and Jordyn?

4. How did this story make you feel?

5. What do you think the author was trying to explain in the story?

6. What part of the story do you think you will remember the most?

7. If the author were to write another book using the same characters, what do you think it would be about?

8. How do you think you would react if that happened to you?

9. Parents/Kids, tell us what you think after you read.

Like our Facebook and message us your answers to the questions listed above.

https://www.facebook.com/djpfamilyproductions/

Please visits our website at
www.DJPFamilyProductions.com

Like us on
https://www.facebook.com/djpfamilyproductions/

Made in the USA
Columbia, SC
08 July 2024